85563

E   Punnett, Dick
PUN   Double-rhyme--
           Peek-a-boo Sue

DOUBLE-RHYME
Peek-a-boo Sue

by Dick Punnett
illustrated by
Tom Dunnington

THE
CHILD'S
WORLD

MANKATO, MN 56001

Library of Congress Cataloging in Publication Data

Punnett, Richard Douglas.
  Peek-a-boo Sue.

  (Double-rhyme books)
  Summary: The birth of a baby kangaroo revitalizes the
zoo at Malibu.
  1. Children's stories, American.   [1. Kangaroos—
Fiction.   2. Zoos—Fiction.   3. Stories in rhyme]
I. Dunnington, Tom.   II. Title.   III. Series.
PZ8.3.P97Pe 1985   [E]   84-23003
ISBN 0-89565-305-2

DOUBLE-RHYME

Peek-a-boo Sue

To Jessie Punnett, my favorite Aunt!

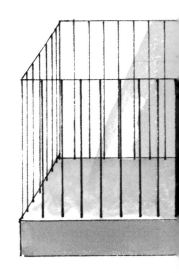

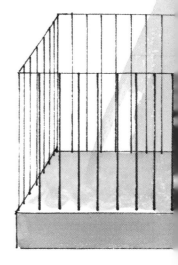

No one went to the Malibu Zoo.
There was not much to see,
and not much to do.

There was a lion, a camel,
and a caribou too,

and just one more,
named Kangaroo Sue.
That was all there were,
and that was just too few.

So up for sale went
the Malibu Zoo!

But look what happened
to Kangaroo Sue.

Up from her pouch popped
a brand new Sue!

Then down she ducked
to hide from you too …

but popped up again,
to peek-a-boo you!

My, how she tickled
the whole zoo crew!
They quickly named
her "Peek-a-boo Sue"!

The word spread fast!
And a news crew flew

straight to the zoo,
to interview Sue!

So she got on TV! And the
next thing you knew,

people came running
to the Malibu Zoo!

So many came that
the whole zoo crew

started to build a
brand new zoo.

They built a cage where
a cockatoo flew

and bought a moose
and a kinkajou too.

My, oh my, how the new
zoo grew!

But the star of the show
was Peek-a-boo Sue!

So all together, let's sing to Sue,
and everything she does,

you do too. Peek-a, peek-a
Peek-a-boo Sue ...

down,

then UP, to peek-a-boo you!!

Peek-a, peek-a, peek-a-boo Sue,
down, then UP, to peek-a-boo you.

About the Author:

Dick Punnett grew up in Penfield, New York, and graduated from Principia College in Elsah, Illinois. After further studies at the Art Center School and Chouinard Art Institute in Los Angeles, he became a writer-cartoonist for a Hollywood animation studio. His current residence is in Ormond Beach, Florida, where he and his wife live along the Tomoka River. Mr. Punnett is the author of the popular Talk-Along books.

About the Artist:

Tom Dunnington hails from the Midwest, having lived in Minnesota, Iowa, Illinois, and Indiana. He attended the John Herron Institute of Art in Indianapolis and the American Academy of Art and the Chicago Art Institute in Chicago. He has been an art instructor and illustrator for many years. In addition to illustrating books, Mr. Dunnington is working on a series of paintings of endangered birds (produced as limited edition prints). His current residence is in Oak Park, Illinois, where he works as a free-lance illustrator and is active in church and community youth work.